POKÉMON

Gotta catch 'em all!™

OFFICIAL GUIDE TO

LEGENDARY
AND MYTHICAL
POKÉMON

SCHOLASTIC

POKéMON

Gotta catch 'em all!™

OFFICIAL GUIDE TO LEGENDARY AND MYTHICAL POKéMON

By Simcha Whitehill

SCHOLASTIC INC.

Distributed in the UK by: Scholastic UK Ltd, Westfield Road,
Southam, Warwickshire, England CV47 0RA.

Published by Scholastic Inc., *Publishers since 1920.* SCHOLASTIC and
associated logos are trademarks and/or registered trademarks of
Scholastic Inc.

The publisher does not have any control over and does not assume any
responsibility for author or third-party websites or their content.

This book is a work of fiction. Names, characters, places, and incidents are
either the product of the author's imagination or are used fictitiously, and
any resemblance to actual persons, living or dead, business establishments,
events, or locales is entirely coincidental.

ISBN 978-1-338-11291-7

12 11 10 9 8 7 6   16 17 18 19 20

Printed in the U.S.A.   40
First printing 2016

Book design by Kay Petronio

CONTENTS

MEET THE LEGENDARY AND MYTHICAL POKÉMON!

The incredible Legendary and Mythical Pokémon you'll discover in this book are straight out of the pages of Pokémon legends. They're incredibly strong, far beyond even the most skilled Pokémon—and that is why they have had so much influence. They are Pokémon who have used their power to shape history and, in some cases, the world.

These Pokémon roam Kanto, Johto, Hoenn, Sinnoh, Unova, and Kalos. They are so rare that very few people have ever caught a glimpse of one of them. But we're about to give you an inside look. So what are you waiting for? Turn the page and meet them all!

LEGENDARY & MYTHICAL POKÉMON OF KANTO

THE LEGENDARY

ARTICUNO

THE FREEZE POKÉMON

Height
5' 7"

Weight
122.1 LBS.

Type
ICE-FLYING

Articuno is known as the Freeze Pokémon, and it can really ice out a foe. This Legendary Pokémon is so powerful that it can fly just by waving its long ribbon tail.

When Articuno flaps its wings, the air turns chilly. This Legendary Pokémon often brings snowfall in its wake.

When Ash and his pals were on their way to the Battle Frontier, they found themselves in the middle of a snowstorm on a warm, sunny day. When they looked up, they realized it was all because of Articuno!

BIRDS OF KANTO

MOLTRES

This Legendary Bird can really heat up the weather—and the battlefield! If you spot Moltres, it means winter is done and spring is on its way. Moltres might mean a change in season, but one thing never changes: Fire always follows the wishes and whims of this Legendary Bird.

When Moltres gets hurt, some say it dives into an active volcano and heals itself by bathing in lava. This Legendary Pokémon can give off flames and control fire.

Because of its ability to create an inferno, Moltres's fire ignites the torch at the Pokémon League in Kanto. Ash wanted to be a torchbearer carrying Moltres's flame to the battlefield. He was able to carry the flame, but Team Rocket set up a sinkhole to trap him and take the torch. Fortunately, the president of the torch committee had kept a lantern with Moltres's flame burning, just in case. Even contained in a lamp, Moltres's flame was so powerful that it relit the torch and blasted off Jessie, James, and Meowth, too!

LEGENDARY POKÉMON

THE FLAME POKÉMON

Height
6' 07"

Weight
132.3 LBS.

Type
FIRE-FLYING

ZAPDOS

THE ELECTRIC
POKÉMON

Height
5'03"

Weight
116.0 LBS.

Type
ELECTRIC-
FLYING

When a bolt of lightning hits Zapdos, its power increases. This Legendary Pokémon can bend electricity to its will.

When the weather doesn't call for thunderstorms, Zapdos recharges at a mystical lake at the top of a mountain near Blackthorn City. Years ago, during a rainstorm, an ancient temple possessing a powerful crystal was buried at the bottom of the lake. The crystal's powers seeped into the water, and it draws Electric-types like Zapdos to recharge in the magically strong lake currents.

Ash once brought Pikachu to heal in the lake's banks. After Pikachu's health was restored, Team Rocket swooped in and stole the mythical crystal. Zapdos used all its energy to rid the lake of Jessie, James, Meowth, and their power-sapping machine. But the crystal was accidentally blasted off, too!

Ash and Pikachu battled Team Rocket and returned the crystal to the lake. But even back in its underwater home, the crystal had lost its luster. Zapdos was still weak, so Pikachu bravely transferred a huge Thundershock to restore Zapdos's power. The mighty Electric Pokémon regained its strength and reenergized the crystal.

MEW

Happy-go-lucky Mew is fun to be around, but that doesn't mean you shouldn't take it seriously. This small, pink Pokémon plays a big role in Pokémon genetics.

It is said that within Mew's cells rests the entirety of the Pokémon genetic code. This Mythical Pokémon can turn invisible to keep others from noticing it.

Mew is connected to the universe in a way that is unlike any other Pokémon. It is very sensitive to the environment. When the delicate balance of nature is disrupted, Mew is affected.

Because of its great power and the knowledge it possesses, Mew is a frequent target for villains. Mew's life has been in danger on more than one occasion.

MYTHICAL POKÉMON

THE NEW SPECIES POKÉMON

Height
1' 04"

Weight
8.8 LBS.

Type
PSYCHIC

THE NEW SPECIES POKÉMON

Height: *6' 07"*
Weight: *269.0 LBS.*
Type: *PSYCHIC*

MEGA MEWTWO X

GENETIC POKÉMON

Height: *7' 07"*
Weight: *280.0 LBS.*
Type: *PSYCHIC-FIGHTING*

MEGA MEWTWO Y

GENETIC POKÉMON

Height: *4' 11"*
Weight: *72.8 LBS.*
Type: *PSYCHIC*

MEWTWO

MEGA MEWTWO X   MEGA MEWTWO Y

MEWTWO

Scientists created Mewtwo by manipulating its genes. If only they could have given it a sense of compassion . . .

Mewtwo is amazingly powerful, but also extremely dangerous. Humans created Mewtwo's body, but they failed to give it a heart.

LEGENDARY & MYTHICAL POKÉMON OF JOHTO

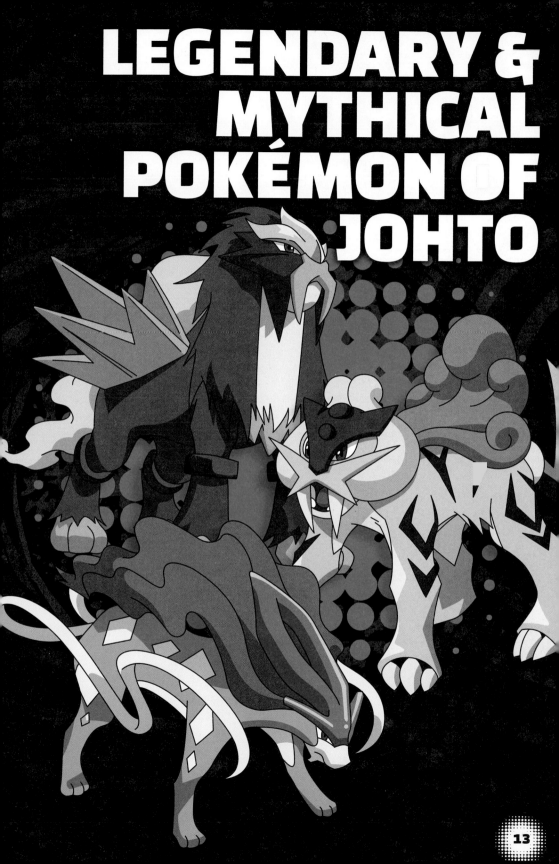

HO-OH

When Ho-Oh's feathers catch the light at different angles, they glow in a rainbow of colors. Legend says these feathers bring joy to whoever holds one.

On Ash's first day as a Trainer, he and Pikachu were caught in a huge thunderstorm. When it cleared, their incredible friendship was solidified. A rainbow appeared in the sky, and Ash thought he saw a Legendary Ho-Oh fly by.

But even a Pokémon that symbolizes so much light and joy can experience darkness. Once upon a time, an evil king of ancient Pokélantis tried to harness Ho-Oh's special power to conquer the world. Instead, Pokélantis was completely destroyed, and the king's spirit was trapped in an orb. When Ash and his pals stumbled on the ancient ruin of Pokélantis, the evil king's spirit decided to possess Ash. But Ash's will was so strong that he was able to snap out of the spell.

In celebration of Ash's victory over the evil king, Ho-Oh flew across the sky. Seeing the Legendary Pokémon again brought back sweet memories of Ash's first days as a Trainer.

LEGENDARY POKÉMON

THE RAINBOW POKÉMON

Height
12' 06"

Weight
438.7 LBS.

Type
FIRE-FLYING

CELEBI

THE TIME
TRAVEL
POKÉMON

Height
2' 00"

Weight
11.0 LBS.

Type
PSYCHIC-
GRASS

Celebi traveled back in time to come to this world. According to myth, its presence is a sign of a bright future.

Celebi can travel across, warp, and change time. However, it is said that Celebi will only appear in times of peace.

Celebi is also directly connected to nature. It has a special bond with forests and plays a role in protecting the environment.

LUGIA

Lugia can knock down a house with one flutter of its enormously powerful wings. For the safety of others, this Legendary Pokémon lives at the bottom of the sea.

Lugia is the great guardian of the sea. But its greatest strength might be its amazing telepathy—it can send its thoughts into the minds of others without saying a word.

Ash and his pals met Lugia and its baby when Team Rocket joined forces with Butch and Cassidy to capture baby Lugia for Dr. Namba. Ash and his pals stepped up to save the small but powerful Pokémon, but both Lugia and Ash's crew wound up getting captured, too. But Ash refused to give up. First he gained Lugia's trust, then he called on Pikachu to help fend off Dr. Namba and his evil team. Together, they were able to free both themselves and Lugia.

LEGENDARY POKÉMON

THE DIVING POKÉMON

Height
17' 01"

Weight
476.2 LBS.

Type
PSYCHIC-FLYING

THE LEGENDARY

LEGENDARY POKÉMON

RAIKOU

THE THUNDER POKÉMON

Height
6'03"

Weight
392.4 LBS.

Type
ELECTRIC

When Raikou roars, the air and land shudder. This Legendary Pokémon moves with lightning speed.

When it comes to this Legendary Beast, its bark is not just a scare tactic. It has the skills to back up its booming growl. Raikou is as fast as lightning, and it can fire bolts off the thundercloud-like mane on its back. Because of its connection to weather, you're mostly likely to see Raikou during a lightning storm. But it will be hard to spot because it flashes through the air with incredible leaps.

BEASTS

ENTEI

Where there's smoke, there's fire. In this case, the smoke that billows off Entei's back is definitely a warning. So beware: Entei's Fire-type attacks burn hotter than lava.

People say that Entei came into being when a volcano erupted. This Legendary Pokémon carries the heat of magma in its fiery heart.

Ash and his pals, amazingly enough, spotted Entei in action when a Trainer challenged the wild Legendary Beast to a battle! Although Misdreavus was confident Mean Look would trap Entei, the powerful Pokémon slipped away easily. Entei was gone in a flash, but its stature left a lasting impression on Ash and his friends.

LEGENDARY POKÉMON

THE VOLCANO POKÉMON

Height
6' 11"

Weight
436.5 LBS.

Type
FIRE

SUICUNE

Suicune can clear pollution from lakes and rivers. This Legendary Pokémon's heart is as pure as clear water.

When Suicune gets close to a dirty pool, the water instantly washes over it, leaving it clean and renewed. Since its special gift is so helpful in maintaining the delicate balance of the environment, Suicune is said to travel on the north wind, racing around to see where it is needed. And whether it is nature, people, or Pokémon that need its help, Suicune is always there.

Ash witnessed one of Suicune's amazing rescue missions. In fact, he was the one rescued by the Legendary Beast! When Ash and his friend Paige floated away with a few Drifloon, they were trapped in a bad storm. Luckily, Paige's little sister, Gabby, knew exactly where to find Suicune. Gabby asked Suicune for help, and it leaped right into action. She hopped onto Suicune's back, and the two swooped in to save Ash and Paige from a disastrous fall down a mountain. But before Ash got the chance to thank the Aurora Pokémon, it had already continued its patrol.

LEGENDARY POKÉMON

THE AURORA POKÉMON

Height
6'07"

Weight
412.3 LBS.

Type
WATER

LEGENDARY & MYTHICAL POKÉMON OF HOENN

DEOXYS

From the crystal on its chest, Deoxys can shoot out laser beams. This highly intelligent Pokémon came into being when a virus mutated during a fall from space.

Deoxys has an incredibly intelligent mind—it just isn't inside its head. The crystal in its chest is actually its brain. Deoxys is connected to the Northern Lights, and it appears with the auroras.

On their way to Pewter City, Ash and his friends spotted an unusual aurora. Then their PokéNavs and Poké Balls went on the fritz. They noticed a flock of Altaria and Swablu flying around strangely. So Ash and his friends investigated the electromagnetic disturbance. Their investigation led them to the site where Deoxys's meteor crashed. There they found the Legendary Pokémon, cold and scared and alone in its new land. But with the help of its newfound friends, Deoxys returned to its Normal Forme. The Legendary Pokémon was so happy to have made a few pals in its strange new world, it decided to set out on a journey to make even more!

LEGENDARY POKÉMON

THE DNA POKÉMON

Height
5' 07"

Weight
134.0 LBS.

Type
PSYCHIC

DID YOU KNOW?
Deoxys used to be a Mythical Pokémon. Now it is categorized as Legendary.

JIRACHI

THE WISH POKÉMON

Height
1' 00"

Weight
2.4 LBS.

Type
STEEL-PSYCHIC

This Mythical Pokémon is said to sleep for a thousand years at a time. But when it wakes up, it can make anyone's dreams come true!

According to myth, if you write your wish on one of the notes attached to Jirachi's head and then sing to it in a pure voice, the Pokémon will awaken from its thousand-year slumber and grant your wish.

Once it's awake, Jirachi will spend a whole week ensuring all the wishes on its notes come true. Then it will return to its slumber. But don't think Jirachi is completely unconscious. If it finds itself in danger, it will fight back and destroy a foe without even opening its eyes. Nothing can disturb Jirachi when it's in a deep sleep!

KYOGRE   **PRIMAL KYOGRE**

KYOGRE

Legends say that Kyogre is the sea personified. When it channels the full power of nature, it can raise sea levels with mighty storms. This Pokémon often clashes with Groudon.

    Kyogre is known for having the strength to bring about storms so great, they raise the sea level to new heights that completely swallow land. An ancient legend tells of a time when Kyogre awoke from its deep sleep at the bottom of an ocean trench and brought an unbelievable storm. Massive tidal waves and heavy rain flooded the land. So you may be grumpy when you wake up in the morning, but you've got nothing on this Legendary Pokémon!

THE SEA BASIN POKÉMON

Height: **14' 09"**
Weight: **776.0 LBS.**
Type: **WATER**

PRIMAL KYOGRE

THE SEA BASIN POKÉMON

Height: **32' 02"**
Weight: **948.0 LBS.**
Type: **WATER**

GROUDON   PRIMAL GROUDON

LEGENDARY POKÉMON

CONTINENT POKÉMON

Height: *11'06"*
Weight: *2,094.4 LBS.*
Type: *GROUND*

PRIMAL GROUDON
CONTINENT POKÉMON

Height: *16'05"*
Weight: *2,205.0 LBS.*
Type: *GROUND-FIRE*

GROUDON

Legends say that Groudon is the land personified. When it channels the full power of nature, it can expand the landmass with eruptions of magma. This Pokémon often clashes with Kyogre.

Weighing in at over one ton, Groudon is quite possibly the heaviest Legendary Pokémon. And it likes to throw its weight around! The Continent Pokémon has the ability to use its hot magma to evaporate the ocean and expand the land. According to legend, Groudon fell into a deep sleep after an intense battle with Kyogre.

RAYQUAZA

Legends say the ancient Pokémon Rayquaza flies through the upper atmosphere and feeds on meteoroids. It's known for stopping the endless battles between Kyogre and Groudon.

Rayquaza has a never-ending appetite for doing what's right. It's the only one who can stop Kyogre and Groudon from fighting and restore order. No one is quite sure when the battle between them began, but Rayquaza is said to be hundreds of millions of years old. Can you imagine how big a birthday cake would have to be to hold that many candles?

THE SKY HIGH POKÉMON

Height: *23'00"*
Weight: *455.2 LBS.*
Type: *DRAGON-FLYING*

MEGA RAYQUAZA
THE SKY HIGH POKÉMON

Height: *35'05"*
Weight: *864.0 LBS.*
Type: *DRAGON-FLYING*

RAYQUAZA   **MEGA RAYQUAZA**

THE EON DUO

LATIOS

Latios can project images into someone else's mind to share information. When it folds its forelegs back against its body, it could beat a jet plane in a race through the sky.

Latios can understand people when they speak, but it is particular about whom it opens up to. It will only converse with caring Trainers. And Latios would rather use its ability to reason than its might. Latios does not like to fight.

Ash had the rare opportunity to take on the battle-shy Latios. In the semifinal round of the Sinnoh League, Ash was matched up against Tobias. Tobias battled Latios next against Ash's Sceptile, and with one great Giga Impact, Sceptile was unable to battle.

Next, Ash called on Swellow. But Latios quickly ended the round with Luster Purge. Then Ash called on Pikachu. Latios's Light Screen cut the strength of Pikachu's attacks in half. Pikachu unleashed a combination of Volt Tackle and Iron Tail so strong that it matched the intensity of Latios's Luster Purge. The sheer force of their attacks left both Pikachu and Latios unable to battle. Tobias was declared the winner in the match against Ash, but Ash was proud of his pal Pikachu for his incredible flair in battle with the Legendary Latios.

LEGENDARY POKÉMON

THE EON POKÉMON

Height: **6' 07"**
Weight: **132.3 LBS.**
Type: **DRAGON-PSYCHIC**

MEGA LATIOS
THE EON POKÉMON

Height: **7' 07"**
Weight: **154.3 LBS.**
Type: **DRAGON-PSYCHIC**

LATIOS　　　　**MEGA LATIOS**

LATIAS MEGA LATIAS

LATIAS

Sensitive and intelligent, Latias can pick up on people's emotions and understand what they're saying. The down that covers its body can refract light to change its appearance.

You don't have to say a word to Latias. It can read your feelings telepathically. So if you've come to cause trouble, beware. Latias will sense it coming, ruffle its feathers, and let out shriek so high-pitched that it will intimidate even the toughest opponent.

THE EON POKÉMON

Height: **5' 11"**
Weight: **88.2 LBS.**
Type: **DRAGON-PSYCHIC**

MEGA LATIAS
THE EON POKÉMON

Height: **5' 11"**
Weight: **114.6 LBS.**
Type: **DRAGON-PSYCHIC**

THE LEGENDARY

THE ICEBERG POKÉMON

Height
5'11"

Weight
385.8 LBS.

Type
ICE

REGICE

Created during an ice age, Regice's body is frozen solid, and even lava can't melt it. It can lower the temperature of the air around it by several hundred degrees.

Regice's entire body is made of an ancient ice so cold, it's impossible to melt. Even if Regice jumped into a volcano, the boiling-hot magma would have no effect on its frosty frame. It lives in a state of deep freeze at -328 degrees Fahrenheit.

REGIROCK

Regirock's body is made entirely of rocks, and these rocks were recently discovered to be from all around the world. It repairs itself after battle by seeking out new rocks.

If this Legendary Pokémon is damaged during battle, it can fill in the gap with any rock it finds.

THE ROCK PEAK POKÉMON

Height
5' 07"

Weight
507.1 LBS.

Type
ROCK

REGISTEEL

**THE IRON
POKÉMON**

**Height
6'03"**

**Weight
451.9 LBS.**

**Type
STEEL**

Registeel isn't actually made of steel—it's a strange substance harder than any known metal. Ancient people sealed it away in a prison.

After living underground for thousands of years, the metal on Registeel's body became so compressed that researchers aren't quite sure of what exactly its body is composed. Amazingly enough, the leading theory is that the metal in Registeel's body cannot be found anywhere on Earth. It's completely unique, and its origin is unknown. The material is so strong that, although the Legendary Pokémon is completely hollow, its metal is indestructible. Nothing can crush it or even scratch the surface.

THE BATTLE TO PROTECT FOUR LEGENDARY POKÉMON

Ash, Brock, Dawn, Piplup, and Pikachu were visiting Frontier Brain Brandon's Battle Pyramid when a surprise visitor drove up—Maria, the local Snowpoint Temple guardian.

"Brandon, a mysterious group of people has surrounded the entrance to the temple!" Maria cried.

"Let's board the Battle Pyramid and head there right away," Brandon replied.

Eager to volunteer, Ash and his friends joined Brandon in the Battle Pyramid as it took flight. Maria began to tell them the history of her beloved Snowpoint Temple.

"Legend has it," she said, "that a long time ago, a fiery volcano erupted and swallowed Snowpoint Forest in its inferno, reducing all the rich greenery to ash. As its lava flowed downhill, it became clear its path of destruction was headed straight for Snowpoint City.

"Out of the darkness, a bright blue light shone like a beacon, bringing with it the Legendary Pokémon Regigigas. Along with Regirock, Registeel, and Regice, Regigigas stopped the ferocious volcano from destroying another step. Together, the four Legendary Pokémon saved the entire city from complete ruin!

"Then Regigigas transformed itself into a round blue stone filled with light. Inside its orb form, it fell into a deep slumber. To protect the sleeping giant, Regirock, Regice, and Registeel transformed themselves into guardian pillars made of the three basic elements of the land: rock, ice, and steel. Snowpoint Temple stands above the spot where these magical shifts took place. The Legendary Pokémon have remained there for centuries, safe and sound. Until now . . ."

As the Battle Pyramid neared the temple, Brandon spotted the source of the trouble—Hunter J, the Pokémon poacher, and her henchmen. Hunter J had set her sights on catching the Legendary Regigigas.

Before Brandon and his Battle Pyramid crew could make a move, Hunter J sent swarms of Metang and Skarmory to attack them in midair.

Whap!

Bam!

Pop!

The Battle Pyramid was trapped in a hail of a hundred slimy Sludge Bombs and fiery Flash Canons!

One of the rotors on the Battle Pyramid snapped. "Hang on, everyone!" Brandon shouted, steering into an emergency landing.

The Battle Pyramid hit the ground with a thud and slid to a slow stop. Everyone piled into Brandon's minicraft to get closer to the temple.

"They're back!" one of Hunter J's goons cried, watching the minicraft approach. "Prepare for another attack!"

Another swarm of Metang and Skarmory filled the sky, ready to strike again. But before they could make the first move, Ash called out, "Pikachu, Thunderbolt, now!"

"Piplup, use Bubblebeam," Dawn added.

Together, their attacks cleared a path to the temple doors. Ash and his friends ran inside to the altar, where they came face-to-face with Hunter J. She proudly showed off the destruction of the temple—the rocky rubble of what once were the pillars of Regice and Regirock. With her powerful Salamence doing her bidding, J would stop at nothing to destroy the Legendary Guardians and awaken Regigigas.

"You must not go through with this," Maria pleaded. "Disturbing Regigigas could lead to disaster!"

"Pfft." Hunter J shrugged, signaling Salamence to strike again.

With a quick blast of Hyper Beam, Salamence made Registeel's pillar smash down on the path to the altar, blocking Ash and his crew from getting closer.

"All you can do now is stand and watch," Hunter J said, smirking.

Salamence fired off a series of Flamethrowers on Regigigas's blue stone.

Suddenly, powerful red light beamed up from a triangle carving in the floor. Regigigas announced itself with an angry roar. It started firing attacks at the temple walls. The whole sacred place began to crumble.

"Regigigas, you've got to stop!" Ash warned, dodging a boulder.

But there was no reasoning with the furious giant.

"Intense rage is making it go berserk!" Maria cried.

Everyone inside the temple raced to avoid the rain of rocks falling from Regigigas's brutal blasts. Even Hunter J and Salamence were forced to retreat.

Brandon called on Regirock, Registeel, and Regice to protect the crew while they raced away. With the help of the Legendary Pokémon, the friends escaped.

Boom! The entire temple collapsed into one big pile of rocks. With a single rage-filled blast, Regigigas broke free and went on a rampage!

Brandon thought the only way to stop the Colossal Pokémon was to catch it. So he had Regirock, Registeel, and Regice launch a coordinated attack of Hyper Beam and Focus Punch. But their triple attack was no match for the massive Pokémon.

"It stopped the three of them with one hit!" Dawn exclaimed.

Brandon asked Regice to freeze Regigigas in Ice Beam. The massive Pokémon turned into an iceberg.

"You did it!" Ash cheered.

But Regigigas' rage was so strong that it crushed its ice coat into ice cubes. Regice, Registeel, and Regirock snapped back into battle action!

Hunter J swooped in on Salamence and had Ariados tie up Brandon and the crew with sticky String Shot.

"No way, Hunter J!" Ash shouted.

Suddenly, the Colossal Pokémon surprised everyone with Confuse Ray. And Regirock, Registeel, and Regice began following instruction from Regigigas! The three fired attacks at J until she was forced to retreat again.

"It's just like the legend! They've become the three pillars that protect Regigigas!" Maria exclaimed.

But the blasts continued as the four Legendary Pokémon marched away, firing in every direction, leaving a path of rocky rubble in their wake. They were heading straight for town!

"If we don't stop them, it will be a disaster!" Brock worried.

The crew was still struggling to break out of Ariados's String Shot. *"Croagunk!"* Brock's Pokémon pal shouted, bursting out of its Poké Ball.

Croagunk quickly freed its Trainer, who helped his friends get out of their sticky shackles. Then they got back in Brandon's minicraft to search for the rampaging Regigigas, Regirock, Registeel, and Regice.

They weren't the only ones looking for the Legendary Pokémon. Hunter J and her goons had set up a trap in a mountain pass. When Regigigas was in sight, Hunter J had one of her henchmen fire at the ground around its feet. Then the ship shot gobs of glue to net the Colossal Pokémon.

Regirock, Registeel, and Regice stepped up to protect Regigigas from another attack.

"Get out of my way!" Hunter J yelled, firing from her wrist cannon.

Ash and his crew arrived just in time to see Hunter J's blasts turn Registeel and Regice to stone. But before J could hit Regirock, Brandon jumped in front of her fire to protect the Legendary Pokémon. Instantly, he turned into rock, too!

"Oh, no, Brandon!" Ash cried out.

Regigigas gazed down at Brandon. The Legendary Pokémon suddenly realized that Brandon and his crew had been trying to protect it.

"You meddlesome fools!" Hunter J shouted, pointing her wrist cannon at them.

When Regigigas realized his new friends were in jeopardy, he gained the strength to break free from Hunter J's glue trap. It stepped in front of Hunter J's destructive blast and protected Ash and his crew.

Sensing the tide had turned against her, Hunter J packed up her goons and hurried away.

But though the battle had ended, Brandon, Regice, and Registeel were still trapped in stone, and Ash and his pals didn't know how to free them.

"Brock, isn't there any way for us to return all of them back to normal?" Ash asked.

"I don't know . . ." Brock admitted.

"Regigigas, forgive us please!" Maria begged. "I'm sorry we weren't able to protect your slumber. But I promise, we did our best to save you. Can you save them now?"

Regigigas nodded, ready to help. He bathed the rock figures in the blue glow of Hidden Power. The stone melted away, and Registeel, Regice, and Brandon were free!

"Regigigas, are you okay?" Brandon asked.

Regigigas nodded. Whatever was left of its rage disappeared. Before the friends' eyes, Regigigas again returned to its round blue stone form.

"Regigigas's slumber will never be disturbed again!" Brandon vowed.

Brandon promised to fulfill the legend and have Regirock, Regice, and Registeel return to their rightful places as guardian pillars to protect Regigigas. As for Ash and his friends, they were happy to have helped restore both faith and the safety of the Legendary Pokémon.

LEGENDARY & MYTHICAL POKÉMON OF SINNOH

THE GRATITUDE POKÉMON

LAND FORME

Height
0' 08"

Weight
4.6 LBS.

Type
GRASS

SHAYMIN

Shaymin can take on two formes—Land and Sky. Shaymin Land Forme is shy, while Shaymin Sky Forme is spunky. But despite their personality differences, they share the same power. Shaymin can completely restore a land destroyed by pollution.

When the Gracidea flower blooms, Shaymin gains the power of flight. Wherever it goes, it clears the air of toxins and brings feelings of gratitude.

Ash and his pals once had the chance to see a Land Forme Shaymin transform into Sky Forme Shaymin. Deep in the forest, they meet Marley, a girl caring for a sick Shaymin. Ash and his crew were happy to help her restore its health. They found a field with blooming Gracidea flowers, which helped Shaymin shift into Sky Forme. The Mythical Pokémon gained wings—and the confidence to fly away on its own journey to spread Gracidea flowers across the land.

THE ALPHA
POKÉMON

Height
10' 06"

Weight
705.5 LBS.

Type
NORMAL

ARCEUS

In the mythology of the Sinnoh region, Arceus emerged from its Egg into complete nothingness, and then shaped the world and everything in it.

For this reason, Arceus is known as the creator— and it is called the Alpha Pokémon.

MANAPHY

From its earliest days, Manaphy possesses the power to form close bonds with any Pokémon, no matter what kind.

Manaphy is truly amazing at making friends. And its gift with emotions also extends into empathy. It can help people change their minds by showing them what it's like to be on the other side of an issue using Heart Swap.

Manaphy does not shy away from its responsibility to the community. It often acts as the leader of the Pokémon in the ocean. That's why it's called the Prince of the Sea.

MYTHICAL POKÉMON

THE SEAFARING POKÉMON

Height
1' 00"

Weight
3.1 LBS.

Type
WATER

THE SEA
DRIFTER
POKÉMON

Height
1' 04"

Weight
6.8 LBS.

Type
WATER

PHIONE

Phione gather in large groups as they drift with the current through warm seas. After floating for a time, they always return home, no matter how far they have traveled.

When the water is warm, Phione's head will inflate like a pool float, letting the Mythical Pokémon flow with the ocean's currents.

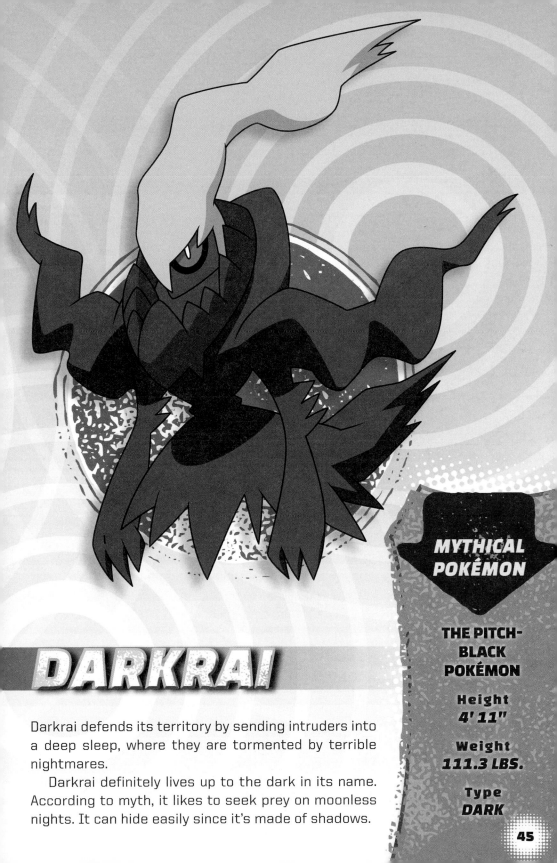

DARKRAI

Darkrai defends its territory by sending intruders into a deep sleep, where they are tormented by terrible nightmares.

Darkrai definitely lives up to the dark in its name. According to myth, it likes to seek prey on moonless nights. It can hide easily since it's made of shadows.

MYTHICAL POKÉMON

THE PITCH-BLACK POKÉMON

Height
4'11"

Weight
111.3 LBS.

Type
DARK

CRESSELIA

The glimmering particles that trail from Cresselia's wings resemble a veil. This Legendary Pokémon, which brings happy dreams, is said to be a symbol of the crescent moon.

Cresselia's joy is the only thing that can balance the darkness that Darkrai brings. Ash and his friends learned firsthand just how Darkrai's grip could ruin a good night's sleep. When they visited Canalave City, they discovered all the locals had been suffering from nightmares. Darkrai typically visited the city once a year, and a Cresselia from Full Moon Island shooed it away after a one-night stay. But this year, Darkrai came early, and Cresselia was missing.

Ash and his friends volunteered to help Officer Jenny track down Cresselia. Dawn called on Swinub, who sniffed its way to a cliff where Cresselia's shrine stood. The Legendary Pokémon appeared—but so did Team Rocket. Swinub battled back the trio of villains with such passion that it evolved into Piloswine!

Once free, Cresselia headed to Canalave City to challenge Darkrai to a battle. But the Pitch-Black Pokémon was a coward. It backed down and ran out of town. Knowing the city was safe to sleep again, Cresselia bid Ash, Dawn, and their friends farewell.

LEGENDARY POKÉMON

THE LUNAR POKÉMON

Height
4'11"

Weight
188.7 LBS.

Type
PSYCHIC

GIRATINA

As punishment, the Legendary Pokémon Giratina was banished to another dimension, where everything is distorted and reversed.

This other dimension is a strange place with low gravity. Giratina is the only one who is free to travel between the Reverse World and the normal world. These two worlds are linked. When time and space are damaged, the Reverse World corrects the damage. But if Giratina sees someone cause lots of damage to time and space, it will chase down the offender!

LEGENDARY POKÉMON

THE RENEGADE POKÉMON

Height
22' 08"

Weight
1,433.0 LBS.

Type
GHOST-DRAGON

THE LAVA DOME
POKÉMON

Height
5'07"

Weight
948.0 LBS.

Type
FIRE-STEEL

HEATRAN

Some like it hot, and Heatran is definitely that type! Said to have been born from fire, Heatran's blood boils like lava.

Heatran makes its home in caves carved out by volcanic eruptions. This Legendary Pokémon's feet can dig into rock, allowing it to walk on walls and ceilings.

DIALGA

It is said Dialga can control time with its mighty roar. In ancient times, it was revered as a legend.

According to legend, time began when Dialga was born. Because of its incredible relationship to every second, Dialga has complete control over clocks. The Temporal Pokémon can bend any instant to its will with its mighty Roar of Time.

THE TEMPORAL POKÉMON

Height
17' 09"

Weight
1,505.8 LBS.

Type
STEEL-DRAGON

49

THE SPATIAL
POKÉMON

Height
13' 09"

Weight
740.8 LBS.

Type
**WATER-
DRAGON**

50

PALKIA

It is said Palkia can cause rents and distortions in space. In ancient times, it was revered as a legend.

There are shrines to Dialga and Palkia all over Sinnoh. According to ancient legends, Palkia lives in a parallel dimension. Because it does not visit the Pokémon world often, not much is known about it. However, it is said that this Legendary Pokémon can morph and mold space.

REGIGIGAS

According to legend, Regigigas built smaller models of itself out of rock, ice, and magma. It's so enormous that it could tow an entire continent behind it.

Regigigas has a connection to three Pokémon called Regirock, Registeel, and Regice. They have different types, but these Pokémon are like Regigigas in many ways. All of them have robotic voices and flashing lights on their bodies. And all are found in old and forgotten places.

THE COLOSSAL POKÉMON

Height
12' 03"

Weight
925.9 LBS.

Type
NORMAL

THE LAKE

**THE
WILLPOWER
POKÉMON**

**Height
1' 00"**

**Weight
0.7 LBS.**

**Type
PSYCHIC**

AZELF

According to legend, Azelf brought a lasting balance to the world. It is known as "the Being of Willpower."

Legendary Pokémon Azelf, Mesprit, and Uxie were hatched from the same egg. Azelf is known for a special gift: It brought an enduring balance to the world. To keep this delicate balance without disruption, Azelf sleeps at the bottom of a lake.

GUARDIANS

MESPRIT

According to legend, Mesprit brought the first taste of joy and sorrow to people's hearts. It is known as "the Being of Emotion."

Mesprit taught people happiness, sadness, and even pain. Those emotions have added a complex and wonderful depth to life. Like Azelf, it sleeps at the bottom of a lake, but it is said that sometimes its spirit rises and flies across the lake's surface.

LEGENDARY POKÉMON

THE EMOTION POKÉMON

Height
1' 00"

Weight
0.7 LBS.

Type
PSYCHIC

**THE
KNOWLEDGE
POKÉMON**

**Height
1'00"**

**Weight
0.7 LBS.**

**Type
PSYCHIC**

UXIE

According to legend, Uxie brought the gift of intelligence to humankind. It is known as "the Being of Knowledge."

But beware: Uxie can take intelligence away, too! Legends say that if you stare into its eyes, it can wipe out your memory.

LEGENDARY & MYTHICAL POKÉMON OF UNOVA

THE SWORDS OF

COBALION

THE IRON WILL POKÉMON

Height
6' 11"

Weight
551.2 LBS.

Type
STEEL-FIGHTING

Like its body, Cobalion's heart is tough as steel. Legends say that in the past, it protected Pokémon from harmful people.

Cobalion's glare is even tougher than its body. With one look, Cobalion can get even the most out-of-control Pokémon to settle down. It cannot stand rudeness or disrespect. So it will remind any Pokémon—or any person, for that matter—to mind its manners. In fact, according to ancient tales, Cobalion has been known to protect Pokémon from human bullies.

JUSTICE

VIRIZION

According to legend, Virizion can move so swiftly that its opponents are left bewildered. Its horns are lovely and graceful—and as sharp as blades.

You just might miss this Legendary Pokémon as it whizzes past you! Watching Virizion move is like trying to follow the wind. If the Grassland Pokémon chooses to stay in one place, it can mow a foe down with its horns.

THE CAVERN
POKÉMON

Height
6' 03"

Weight
573.2 LBS.

Type
ROCK-FIGHTING

TERRAKION

Legends tell of a time when Terrakion attacked a mighty castle to protect its Pokémon friends. They say it knocked down a giant wall with the force of its charge.

Although it might look like it's all brawn, Terrakion actually has a big heart. It has a soft spot for any Pokémon in need. When a human war forced a group of Pokémon from their peaceful homes, Terrakion stepped in to save them.

KELDEO

Keldeo travels the world visiting beaches and river-banks, where it can race across the water. When this Mythical Pokémon is filled with resolve, it gains a blinding speed.

The Colt Pokémon is so swift that it's actually hard to see. When it's determined, its body fills with a strong power that increases its speed. Its great leaps become impossible to follow with the naked eye.

MYTHICAL POKÉMON

THE COLT POKÉMON

Height
4' 07"

Weight
106.9 LBS.

Type
WATER-FIGHTING

THE PALEOZOIC POKÉMON

Height
4'11"

Weight
181.9 LBS.

Type
BUG-STEEL

GENESECT

The powerful cannon on Genesect's back is the result of Team Plasma's meddling. This Mythical Pokémon is 300 million years old.

The ancient bug Pokémon was just a fossil . . . until evil Team Plasma got their hands on it. They brought Genesect back to life, and they also changed it forever.

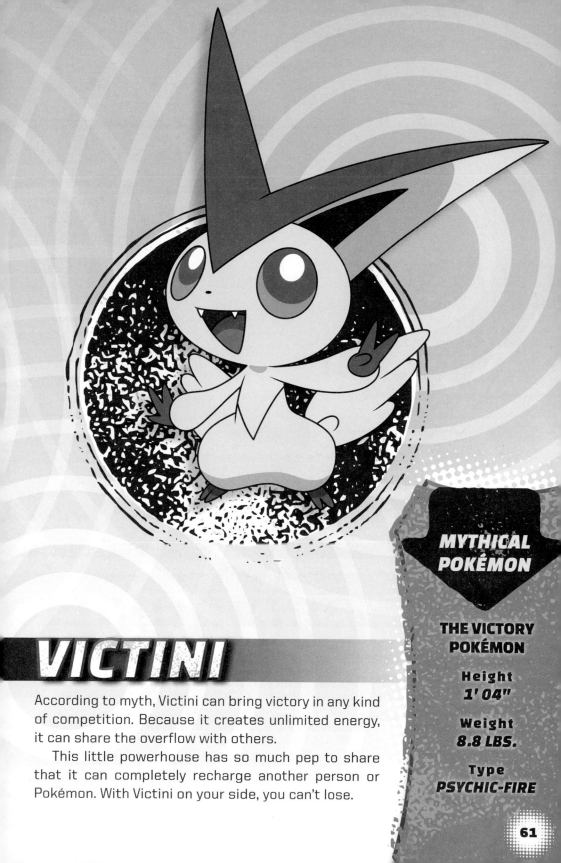

VICTINI

According to myth, Victini can bring victory in any kind of competition. Because it creates unlimited energy, it can share the overflow with others.

This little powerhouse has so much pep to share that it can completely recharge another person or Pokémon. With Victini on your side, you can't lose.

MYTHICAL POKÉMON

THE VICTORY POKÉMON

Height
1' 04"

Weight
8.8 LBS.

Type
PSYCHIC-FIRE

LEGENDARY POKÉMON

THUNDURUS

THE BOLT STRIKE POKÉMON

Height
4' 11"

Weight
134.5 LBS.

Type
ELECTRIC-FLYING

Thundurus can discharge powerful electric bolts from the spikes on its tail. This Legendary Pokémon causes terrible lightning storms, which often result in forest fires.

This Legendary Pokémon has started some pretty legendary blazes. So be sure to look out for fierce lightning if you're below this prickly Pokémon.

NATURE

TORNADUS

Wrapped in its cloud, Tornadus flies at 200 MPH. This Legendary Pokémon causes fierce windstorms with gales that can knock down houses.

While Tornadus might blow by in an instant, its power over air can create lasting damage. With the tap of its tail, Tornadus can cover the land with a wild wind. With a little release of energy, it can create a big storm. With a whistle, Tornadus can blow a breeze so tough it will topple the buildings below.

THE CYCLONE POKÉMON

Height
4' 11"

Weight
138.9 LBS.

Type
FLYING

LEGENDARY POKÉMON

LANDORUS

THE ABUNDANCE POKÉMON

Height
4' 11"

Weight
149.9 LBS.

Type
GROUND-FLYING

Because its arrival helps crops grow, Landorus is welcomed as "the Guardian of the Fields." This Legendary Pokémon uses the energy of wind and lightning to enrich the soil.

Although Landorus soars in the sky, it has an incredible power over the land. No matter where the plot of dirt or what its condition, Landorus can transform it into an incredible spot for crops with its arrival. Using its tail, it will greatly fertilize any field and help it yield a beautiful bounty. The crop will grow taller than any planted by hand, and it will rise up almost instantly.

THE RAGE AND REVIVAL OF LEGENDS

Ash and his friends Iris and Cilan were visiting Milos Island in search of Revival Herbs needed to restore injured Pokémon to health. But when they arrived, their guide, Lewis, informed them that all the Revival Herbs he could find were dried out—and his Pokémon were getting sick! There was one Revival Herb left in his stock.

Lewis was determined to bring the land back to life. He planned to lead a special Rainmaking Ceremony with his Pokémon, Gothorita, the next day. Ash, Iris, and Cilan eagerly agreed to take part.

So Lewis began to tell them the legend of Milos Island . . .

Long ago, Thundurus and Tornadus were locked in an epic battle. Landorus bravely stepped in to stop their fighting and was horribly wounded. The ancient people of Milos Island used Revival Herbs to help

the Legendary Pokémon recover. It regained its strength and was able to break up the battle. To thank the people who had healed it, Landorus turned Milos Island into a paradise full of Revival Herbs.

The next morning, the kids headed to the Shrine of Landorus, a big stone pillar covered in ancient carvings.

"Landorus!" Lewis called out. "The Revival Herbs have all dried up. We ask for rain for Milos Island!"

Lewis's Gothorita echoed his words with a song. Its voice created a pink glow that traveled up into the clouds.

Suddenly, a giant dark cloud took form. At first it looked like rain, but then a strange shape appeared in the sky. Out of the clouds emerged the Legendary Pokémon Tornadus! It sent back-to-back attacks of Hurricane and Air Slash.

"Look out!" Iris warned. "Why is Tornadus so angry?"

"Something happened to Tornadus's stone-pillar home," Lewis replied.

Ash, Lewis, and Iris hurried away to investigate. Soon they found Tornadus's stone had been smashed! Now there was nothing to stop the rage of the Cyclone Pokémon.

"Who could have done such a thing?" Lewis wondered.

Worse yet, the friends discovered Thundurus's stone pillar had also been smashed. There were two angry Legendary Pokémon on the loose!

"*Thuuuundurus!*" Thundurus shouted.

"*Torrrrrnaaaaadus!*" Tornadus yelled back.

The two began to fight each other, just like in the Legend of Milos Island.

"The battle between Tornadus and Thundurus is starting all over again!" Lewis realized.

"We've got to stop those two, and fast!" Ash declared.

Snivy shot Leaf Storm. *Pew, pew, pew!*

Excadrill fired Focus Blast. *Wham!*

Axew drummed up Dragon Rage. *Boom!*

Stunfisk released Mud Bomb. *Slap!*

But the Legendary Pokémon easily dodged their attacks. So Lewis asked Gothorita to try reasoning with them.

Gothorita sang the message with all its might, but it only made the Pokémon angrier. Tornadus's wind knocked down trees in the forest. Thundurus's bolts broke rocks right off the mountainside. The Legendary Pokémon were intent on destroying each other, and in the process, they would also destroy Milos Island!

"There's only one thing left to do," Lewis said. "We have to have a Shrine Maiden summon the guardian of Milos Island, Landorus."

"Where are we going to find a Shrine Maiden?" Iris asked.

"Iris, I'm looking right at her!" Lewis replied, smiling.

Once she dressed in traditional Milos Island garb, Iris was ready to give it her all! Lewis came prepared with mysterious stones that increased Gothorita's power.

When they reached the pillar of Landorus, Iris bowed her head. "Landorus, I beg for your help from the bottom of my heart."

Bathed in a pink glow, Gothorita sang her feelings to the shrine. A powerful yellow light shined over the area, and then shot straight up into the sky. The light was absorbed into a figure—Landorus!

"Landorus," Lewis addressed the Legendary Pokémon with respect. "Tornadus and Thundurus are battling so fiercely, they're going to destroy Milos Island! I beg you to stop them!"

"*Landor!*" It nodded, ready to take action.

A bolt of lightning burst through the gray sky, and Landorus followed it to find Tornadus and Thundurus. Landorus pleaded with them to stop their petty fighting.

"*Thundurus!*" the Pokémon replied with a roar, firing Focus Blast.

"*Torrrrrrnadus!*" the other snarled back, shooting Hurricane.

Landorus had convinced Tornadus and Thundurus to stop fighting each other. Instead, they joined forces to attack it!

"It's two against one!" Ash yelped.

Landorus defended itself with a powerful burst of Extrasensory. Tornadus hit back with Hammer Arm, slamming Landorus into a mountainside. Landorus was trapped and under attack as Thundurus threw Focus Blast!

Suddenly, Landorus broke free and launched Hyper Beam. But when Tornadus responded with Hidden Power, it blasted big rocks off the mountainside.

Crash!

"Landorus, behind you!" Lewis cried.

Gothorita jumped in and fired Psyshock to stop Thundurus from its sneak attack.

"*Laaaaaaandoruuuuuuuuus!*" Landorus shouted, sending a burst of Hyper Beam.

Direct hit! While Thundurus and Tornadus tried to recover from the wallop, Landorus again tried to reason with them.

Suddenly, laser lines surrounded the three Legendary Pokémon! The lasers formed a cube cage, locking up the trio.

"*Thunduuuuur!*" Thundurus cried, trying to blast its way out.

But even these powerful Legendary Pokémon couldn't break the bonds of their laser cages.

"Who did that?!" Lewis asked.

"Who? That is the question, indeed," replied James. It was Team Rocket!

"So you're the ones who destroyed the stone shrines!" Lewis said.

"Aren't you smart?!" James said. "And we knew when they arrived, you'd have to summon Landorus."

"Now they all belong to us!" Jessie rejoiced.

"Not as long as we're here," Ash replied. Together, he and Iris and Lewis and Cilan directed their Pokémon to attack.

Roggenrola fired Flash Cannon at the cages. *Whap!*

Emolga threw Hidden Power. *Pow!*

Pansage blasted Solar Beam. *Boom!*

Gothorita added Shadow Ball. *Swish!*

But when the smoke cleared, the three Legendary Pokémon were still in their cages.

Team Rocket hopped in a helicopter and loaded up the three cages.

"Finders keepers, losers weepers," James said, waving good-bye.

"Weep, losers!" Meowth chuckled as the helicopter took off.

But Ash, Iris, Cilan, and Lewis refused give up. They banded together and fired at the helicopter instead of the cages.

So Roggenrola fired Flash Cannon. *Whap!*

Emolga threw Hidden Power. *Pow!*

Pansage blasted Solar Beam. *Boom!*

It worked! The helicopter began to smoke, and Team Rocket had to release the cages from the helicopter.

The three cages fell from the sky, landing in the valley.

"Laaaandorus!" Landorus cried, wincing in pain.

Landorus was injured. It was in no shape to continue fighting, but Tornadus and Thundurus started to attack it again!

Only one thing could save Landorus—the very last Revival Herb.

"Gothorita, send the Revival Herb to Landorus!" Lewis instructed.

Gothorita began to sing again as it used its powerful pink glow to carry the Revival Herbs across the valley to Landorus.

Thundurus and Tornadus launched a coordinated attack to stop it from reaching Landorus.

"Landorus!" it shouted, firing Protect. It received the Revival Herbs!

With its strength restored, Landorus rose back into the sky.

"It's happening exactly like the Milos Island legend!" Cilan exclaimed.

Powerful Landorus finished off Thundurus and Tornadus with a burst of Hyper Beam! Then it again tried to reason with them. With one hand on each of their hearts, Landorus conveyed its hope to restore peace to Milos Island. Gothorita added her song to his plea.

"It looks like Landorus finally got through to them!" Ash said

The dark clouds cleared, and the sun once again shone down on Milos Island. But in the light, Lewis could see the damage the battle had inflicted on the land.

"Landorus, please, heal this island!" Lewis implored. "Return it to its beautiful state so the Revival Herbs can grow again!"

"Landorus!" it promised.

But Landorus couldn't do it all on its own. It needed its legendary brothers Thundurus and Tornadus to restore the delicate balance.

Thundurus brought its power over rain. Tornadus added its power over wind. Landorus brought the Revival Herb seeds. They instantly sprouted up again across the island.

"Wow!" Lewis cried in awe. "Landorus, Tornadus, and Thundurus, thank you!"

"Thank you!" Ash, Iris, and Cilan echoed.

Lewis vowed to continue to take care of Milos Island. As they said good-bye to their new friend, Ash, Iris, and Cilan knew they were leaving it in good hands.

THE
LEGENDARY

**THE
BOUNDARY
POKÉMON**

**Height
9' 10"**

**Weight
716.5 LBS.**

**Type
DRAGON-ICE**

KYUREM

When the freezing energy inside Kyurem leaked out, its entire body froze. Legends say it will become whole with the help of a hero who will bring truth or ideals.

Kyurem itself is never full of hot air—either in its temperatures or lies. Inside its body, this Legendary Pokémon has an icy energy that can freeze out its foes. However, because it can easily spring a leak, Kyurem has accidentally frozen itself over.

UNOVA TRIO

RESHIRAM

**THE VAST WHITE
POKÉMON**

**Height
10' 06"**

**Weight
6,727.5 LBS.**

**Type
DRAGON-FIRE**

Legends say Reshiram is drawn to those who value the truth. The flare of its fiery tail can disrupt the atmosphere and cause strange weather patterns.

Reshiram might look like snow, but it's actually burning hot. In fact, it's white-hot! This Pokémon can start a fierce fire. Reshiram will not hesitate to use its incredible powers to protect those who want to build a world of truth.

THE DEEP
BLACK
POKÉMON

Height
9' 06"

Weight
760.6 LBS.

Type
DRAGON-
FLYING

ZEKROM

Legends say Zekrom helps those who pursue their ideals. It surrounds itself with thunderclouds to travel unseen, and its tail can generate electricity.

Zekrom travels under the cover of dark clouds. It can fire lighting from the electricity in its tail. So, during a storm, you might wonder—is that weather, or is that the Deep Black Pokémon?

Professor Juniper once questioned whether Zekrom was responsible for taking her computer system offline. But even if it gets in tangles with technology, rest assured, Zekrom only has the best of intentions. It will always be there to help anyone who pursues his or her ideals.

MELOETTA

When Meloetta sings, its voice can control the emotions of people or Pokémon. The beautiful melodies of this Mythical Pokémon can bring aching sadness or radiant joy.

Behind Meloetta's sweet sounds is incredible power. Meloetta literally puts emotion in its songs. It can transform the mood of anyone who hears its melodies.

MYTHICAL POKÉMON

THE MELODY POKÉMON

Height
2' 00"

Weight
14.3 LBS.

Type
NORMAL-PSYCHIC

73

MELOETTA & ASH: THE EVOLUTION OF FRIENDSHIP

Ash has a special bond with the Melody Pokémon. Whenever it's in trouble, Ash is there to save the day! But their bond goes both ways. Whenever Ash is in trouble, Meloetta appears. Here's how their friendship evolved . . .

Ash first met Meloetta at Pokéstar Studios in Virbank City. He saved Meloetta from a falling piece of the studio's set. Ash is always ready to help a Pokémon in need, so he didn't think much of the moment. But Meloetta turned into a fan who secretly started following him on his journey.

When Team Rocket saw an opportunity to steal Meloetta, they tossed their electric net. Meloetta escaped, but it rolled down a huge hill and landed in the middle of the road. Luckily, Ash and his friends were just driving by in Cynthia's truck. They immediately stopped and saved the Mythical Pokémon. Using Cynthia's medicine, Ash nursed Meloetta back to health. It flew away, but that wasn't the last Ash and his friends would see or hear of the Melody Pokémon.

Meloetta's voice has a mysteriously powerful strength. When Onix chased after Ash and his friends, they couldn't seem to battle it back. So the Mythical Pokémon began to sing. Upon hearing Meloetta's incredible voice, another brave Onix was so deeply moved that it rose and stopped the other Onix from attacking.

Although Meloetta is terribly timid, it wouldn't miss the chance to root for Ash in the Junior Cup! But even when Ash wasn't competing, Meloetta was always watching over Ash and his friends. Meloetta helped him find shelter and food in the rain. Meloetta also aided Ash across a broken bridge. The Melody Pokémon is as sweet as its song.

LEGENDARY & MYTHICAL POKÉMON OF KALOS

**THE
DESTRUCTION
POKÉMON**

**Height
19' 00"**

**Weight
447.5 LBS.**

**Type
DARK-
FLYING**

YVELTAL

When Yveltal spreads its dark wings, its feathers give off a red glow. It is said that this Legendary Pokémon can absorb the life energy of others.

The crimson light underneath those wings is beautiful to behold, but beware—it might just get a hold of you!

XERNEAS

Xerneas's horns shine in all the colors of the rainbow. It is said that this Legendary Pokémon can share the gift of endless life.

Before Xerneas was reborn, it took the shape of a tree and slept for a whole millennium. After a thousand years of beauty sleep, it's no wonder Xerneas is so special.

THE LIFE POKÉMON

Height
9' 10"

Weight
474.0 LBS.

Type
FAIRY

THE ORDER
POKÉMON

Height
16' 05"

Weight
672.4 LBS.

Type
**DRAGON-
GROUND**

ZYGARDE

Zygarde dwells deep within a cave in the Kalos region. It is said that this Legendary Pokémon is a guardian of the ecosystem.

Zygarde prefers to stay out of sight, but it will appear if the delicate balance of the ecosystem is in trouble.

DIANCIE   MEGA DIANCIE

THE JEWEL
POKÉMON

Height: *2' 04"*
Weight: *19.4 LBS.*
Type: *ROCK-FAIRY*

MEGA DIANCIE
THE JEWEL
POKÉMON

Height: *3' 07"*
Weight: *61.3 LBS.*
Type: *ROCK-FAIRY*

DIANCIE

According to myth, when Carbink suddenly transforms into Diancie, its dazzling appearance is the most beautiful sight in existence. It has the power to compress carbon from the atmosphere, forming diamonds between its hands.

Stunning to behold, this sparkling pink Pokémon's body is covered in bling. It appearance is so unbelievably shiny and so incredibly dazzling, Diancie is said to be the most beautiful Pokémon of all!

HOOPA
CONFINED

HOOPA
UNBOUND

THE MISCHIEF
POKÉMON

Height
1' 08"

Weight
19.8 LBS.

Type
PSYCHIC-
GHOST

HOOPA

Hoopa is heralded as having a huge amount of power. If only it would use it for good instead of greed!

   Hoopa's taste for riches knows no bounds. And with the strength of a Mythical Pokémon, it has the luxury of being able to take what it desires. Hoopa once wanted a royal treasure so badly, it stole the entire castle. Can you imagine carrying a big brick building just to get a few baubles?